Barbara Williamson

Betterflies

Meeting Mariposa

To order additional copies of this book, contact:
Xlibris
844-714-8691
www.Xlibris.com
Orders@Xlibris.com

ISBN: Softcover   978-1-6641-7568-6
        Hardcover   978-1-6641-7569-3
        EBook   978-1-6641-7567-9

Library of Congress Control Number: 2021910557

Print information available on the last page

Rev. date: 09/16/2021

Weto, you make my heart smile! I love you.

I want to thank my dear Prayer Pals—what a blessing you are.
A special thank you to my friend John. You bring smiles to our faces.

Remember FROG — Forever Rely On God!

Chapter 1

Prayer Pals

It was a beautiful spring morning, sun shining, flowers in bloom, and birds singing. As the butterflies, insects, bees, and other animals were beginning their day, you could hear humming, singing, and laughing.

As Mariposa softly landed on a beautiful flower, she saw a caterpillar sleeping under a leaf. She sat quietly for a while, not wanting to wake up the caterpillar. She quietly flew off to meet with her friends.

Mariposa saw her friends sitting on their favorite log. She could hear them laughing. She landed on a branch and said good morning to her friends. Mariposa became friends with four butterflies by sharing their love of God and their faith. The five of them became Prayer Pals.

"Good morning, Prayer Pals. How are all of you doing this beautiful day?" she asked.

Carol replied, "Very well, thank you. I'm enjoying the lovely weather."

Miriam said, "I'm fine, I'm taking time to enjoy the beautiful flowers."

Barb replied, "I'm getting a good amount of flying in. And I really enjoy that."

Susie chimed in, "I am smiling all the time, flying around and enjoying all the colors the flowers provide."

"So ladies, are there any new prayer requests?"

Miriam answered, "Yes, there is a family of dogs that just need some uplifting prayers."

"Oh, how many dogs, Miriam?" asked Susie.

"There are four dogs, but one is really old," answered Miriam.

Then Carol said, "I saw a couple working in their yard, and their yard is on a hill. So how about some sweet safety prayers?"

Barb spoke up, saying, "As we're flying around and able to enjoy our surroundings, let us remember to praise our precious Lord for all our gifts."

"Yes, yes, yes, yes, yes!" all agreed!

The five of them shared stories, laughed, and then ended their morning with prayer. Lifting prayer for the four dogs, and the husband and wife working on the hill.

The Prayer Pals met at least twice a week, once every Sunday for church service, then on Wednesdays for Bible study.

Chapter 2

The Caterpillar

As Mariposa softly landed on a beautiful flower, she saw a caterpillar sleeping under a leaf. She sat quietly for a while, not wanting to wake up the caterpillar. She quietly flew off to meet with other friends.

The next day, Mariposa flew back to where she saw the caterpillar. She landed on the flower she was on before. She looked around and saw some leaves moving. She waited, just watching. Then she saw a head pop up. Then, it was gone again. She flew down to be closer. The head came out again, but this time, there was a shriek. Mariposa said, "I'm sorry, I didn't mean to frighten you."

"Oh, it's okay, everything scares me. Sometimes if I trip over a twig, my own legs scare me. Why are you here?" asked the caterpillar.

"I was here the other day and you were sleeping, I didn't stay because I didn't want to upset your sleep. So I came back today to check on you," she replied.

"Why?" asked the caterpillar.

"Because I care about you," answered the butterfly.

"Why do you care about me?" he replied.

"Because you are my neighbor, and I must love my neighbor as myself," answered Mariposa.

"Thank you for coming back to check on me. Will you come back again?"

"Yes, how about Thursday?" she said.

"Okay, I'll be here," he replied.

A few days later, Mariposa saw her friends, Carol and Miriam, together. She flew down to join them.

"Good morning, Prayer Pals, you make my heart smile," she said.

"Well, thank you. We enjoy seeing you," said Carol.

"So what are you doing today?" asked Miriam.

"A few days ago, I saw a caterpillar all alone. He was sleeping, so I didn't want to scare him, so I flew off. I went back, and yesterday, I met him."

"What's his name, and where does he live?" asked Carol.

"I don't know, and I don't know," replied Mariposa.

"So when will you see him again?" questioned Carol.

"I think today," she replied. "He seems very lonely and sad. I'd just like to spend some time with him

Miriam said, "We can lift him in prayer."

"Yes, we sure will," said Carol.

The three butterflies joined in prayer with uplifting words of encouragement.

Mariposa said her goodbyes and flew off to spend time with the caterpillar.

The caterpillar was lying under some plants, and when he saw the butterfly, he waved. She flew down to be near him.

"Good day," said Mariposa.

"Hello," replied the caterpillar.

"It's a beautiful day. We are so blessed to live here," she said.

"What do you mean?" he questioned.

She replied, "Look around at the beautiful flowers, plants, trees, the sky, and the fresh air. All gifts from God."

The caterpillar said," I don't know who God is. Who is he, and how do you know about him? I'm just a caterpillar, you are a butterfly. Oh, never mind. I'm just glad to see you," moped the sad caterpillar.

"You don't have to be a butterfly to enjoy your life. You can start enjoying your life right now by being a good caterpillar. And I have a feeling, the reason I'm here is to share with you a true story about loving God," said Mariposa.

"Do you have time today to tell me the story?" asked the caterpillar. "But first, you said I don't have to be a butterfly to enjoy my life. What did you mean?"

"Right now, there are things you can enjoy right where you are in life. Such as finding a beautiful leaf or a pretty flower to sleep under. Being able to climb up the stalk of a plant to be in the sunlight or help other animals too tall to reach something down under, or too short to reach something good to eat. Just by being kind and helpful," replied Mariposa.

"Will you show me just what you mean?" said the caterpillar.

"Yes, let's start right now." Mariposa smiled.

The two of them started walking together, and not far from where they began, they saw a little bird with its wing caught in a branch on the ground. Mariposa stopped, waiting for the caterpillar to respond. He looked at her, and she motioned to help. He slowly walked closer to the bird and smiled sweetly. She sadly looked down, but was not afraid. The caterpillar reached with three legs and pulled the branch off the bird's wing. Then he helped the bird bend her wing back. She stood up and flew away, then she waved with her wing, as if thanking him.

He turned and looked at Mariposa with a big smile on his face.

"*Wow*, that was very nice of you to help that bird. How did that feel?" she asked.

"Oh my goodness, that was great. I want to do more," he said.

They continued their walk, and as they did, the caterpillar saw a dog tag in the muddy grass. He thought it wasn't important because it was dirty. He thought no one would care about it.

"So what do you think we should do with this dog tag?" asked Mariposa.

"Well, it's old and dirty. No one would still want it! Right?" questioned the caterpillar.

"Well, we don't know. It might be a favorite tag, it might belong to an old dog. So since we don't know, can you think of something nice to do?" she asked.

"We can wipe it off and put it in a place where others can see it. Is that a good idea?" he asked.

"That's a great idea!" she said.

Together they wiped off the dog tag. It was now easier to read. Together they lifted the tag up where it was easy to see. They both smiled.

"Good work," said the butterfly.

As they turned to walk back to the caterpillar's favorite place, he had a big smile on his face. And then, he looked very sad again.

"What are you thinking? A few minutes ago, you seemed to be so happy, and now, you look so sad," asked the butterfly.

"I was happy when I was outside of myself, helping others. But I don't know how to make myself happy," moped the caterpillar. "I'm lonely. Thank you so much for spending time with me."

"Thank you for sharing your time with me. And today you experienced what I meant by enjoying who you are, just as you are. You saw and helped the bird. You saw the dog tag in the dirt and made it clean and easy to see. And you were happy, helping. Now you need to learn how to love being you," said Mariposa. "We have had a busy day, talking, walking, and helping. I have truly enjoyed our time together. What a blessing." Mariposa smiled.

"What do you mean by a blessing?" he questioned.

"Today you were a blessing to the bird. Also, to have found the dog tag and placed it in plain view for the owner to find. You were a blessing for both of those reasons," she said.

Mariposa bowed her head. "Remember, I said I have a true story to share with you about loving God?"

"Yes." He nodded.

"We have had a full day today, but I promise to come back and share that story with you. I'll return in three days. We can spend the day together," she said.

"Spend the day together, you and me?" He smiled.

"Yes!" She laughed.

Chapter 3

Blessings

On her way home, she saw Susie. Mariposa flew down to talk with her. "Hi, Prayer Pal," Susie said. "What have you been doing this beautiful day?"

"I have been sharing time with the caterpillar," she said. "Today, we talked about blessings. We took a walk, and he helped a bird caught under a branch. Then he found a dog tag in the dirt. We cleaned it and put it in a place easy to see."

"Oh, what a blessing," Susie replied.

"Exactly, except he asked what a blessing was," Mariposa replied.

"So he needs to find the friend he has in Jesus?" Susie nodded.

"Exactly, and we can help him do just that." She smiled back.

Susie and Mariposa said a prayer, asking for sweet words to share with the caterpillar about our Lord. They said their goodbyes. As Mariposa flew away, she waved back at Susie, thanking her.

The next morning, Mariposa flew over to visit with her Prayer Pal Barb.

"Well, good morning, my friend, how are you today?" asked Barb.

"I am well," Mariposa said. "I just wanted to come and talk with you about the caterpillar I've been spending time with.

"Oh my, I would love to be part of sharing our blessing. I'm so grateful for our friendships and our faith bringing us closer and closer together," replied Barb.

"That's exactly what I was thinking. The caterpillar asked me what a blessing is," answered Mariposa.

"Let's talk to our Prayer Pals to join in helping your new friend. Another blessing our Lord has sent to us," Barb replied.

"Barb, are you busy today?" asked Mariposa.

"Never too busy to help a new friend," she answered.

"Oh great. I'll go find Susie, Miriam, and Carol. Let's meet at our favorite prayer log at two. Is that okay?" Mariposa asked.

"Fine with me. I'm excited about it!" replied Barb.

Mariposa flew off to find Carol, who was watching over the couple working on the hill. Carol agreed to join and was really looking forward to hearing more about the caterpillar.

Then Mariposa flew off to find Susie, who was entertaining some children. She was playing hide-and-seek with them. When Susie saw Mariposa, she took time to talk with her. Mariposa explained a little bit about the caterpillar and that the others were meeting to come up with a plan. Susie agreed to join. Just then, they heard a little voice saying, "Nana, can you play with us?"

Susie laughed and told Mariposa, "That's what they call me." And off she flew.

One more stop, Mariposa knew exactly where Miriam would be—watching the dogs. So off Mariposa flew in search of soft-hearted Miriam.

Mariposa flew up to the yard where the dogs lived, and there was Miriam sitting on the fence, watching the dogs play. Miriam was happy to see her friend and excited to hear her news about the caterpillar. She agreed that it was a good idea to join thoughts and come up with a prayer-filled idea to help.

Chapter 4

Prayer Pals Plan

The Prayer Pals flew in one at a time. They landed on their favorite prayer log. They could not stop smiling.

"Okay, friends, we have an important mission ahead of us. As you all know, I met a rather sad caterpillar. He is a soft-spoken, mild-mannered, curious young caterpillar. Let's begin with prayer then think of uplifting faith-filled ideas to share with our new friend."

"Sweet Lord, today let there be peace within us. Let us trust God that we are exactly where we are meant to be. And I believe that friends are quiet angels who lift us to our feet when our wings have trouble remembering how to fly. As Prayer Pals, we ask for kind, uplifting words to share with our new friend," Mariposa prayed. "Amen."

Susie began by saying, "Oh my stars, maybe if we say a favorite Bible verse, then add our thoughts, is that a good way to start? "Yes, everybody, raise your hand if you agree

"Yes, yes, yes, yes, yes!" they all agreed.

Susie began, "'I can do all things through Christ who strengthens me'—Philippians 4:13."

"Oh, Susie, that's perfect!" they all agreed.

"I'll be next," said Barb. "'The Lord is my shepherd, I shall lack nothing'—Psalm 23:1. I was thinking about the sheep that are so well cared for and loved."

"Very nice, Barb," they all agreed.

"May I be next?" said Carol. "'The Lord bless you and keep you. The Lord make his face shine upon you and be gracious to you'—Numbers 6:24–25. Just thinking of our Lord's face looking at us and blessing us continuously is such a blessing."

"Oh, this is so sweet, us revealing our faith so easily," thanked Mariposa.

"Okay, my turn," said Miriam. "'For I know the plans I have for you, declares the Lord, to give you a future and a hope'—Jeremiah 29:11. Two very important gifts our Lord blesses us with."

"I was thinking about John 3:16," said Mariposa. "'For God so loved the world, that he gave his only Son, that whoever believes in him will have eternal life.'"

So now the Prayer Pals continued to talk about things they had experienced — stories about when they were young, about others in their lives that have left valuable time spent, and about faith-filled memories. They came up with a very smart idea: just tell the caterpillar the heartfelt path that Mariposa explained when they first became friends. Then they would invite him to spend time with the Prayer Pals.

Chapter 5

Praying and Trusting

Early Thursday morning, Mariposa said her morning prayers, asking our Lord to give her the right words to share her faith with her new friend. Then she flew off to spend the day with the caterpillar. As she flew to his special place, she saw her Prayer Pals standing together and waving their wings at her.

When she got to the caterpillar's favorite place, he was leaning against a fallen branch so the butterfly could see him easily. And he was waving with four of his legs.

"Good morning, my friend," said Mariposa.

"Yes, it sure is," said the caterpillar. "I have so much to tell you. First, I'm so glad you're here. Thank you for showing me a happier way to live by helping others. I leave in the morning, looking for people to help. And I'm gone all day, but I feel great."

"*Wow*, you've been busy. Congratulations on the new helpful you," said the butterfly.

"But what if I can't find problems to solve? I'll turn back into my lonely, worthless, nothing again," the caterpillar cried. "Maybe this would be a good time to tell me about your friend, God."

"Yes, this is a perfect time to tell you a true, come-to-Jesus story. You get comfortable, and I'll sit right over here.

"Some time ago, there was a young butterfly who was kind of shy and quiet. She called herself 'a not easy to make friends' butterfly. One of her favorite places to stay was on the fence of a friendly old gardener's yard. At first, she would just watch him and fly in the direction he was working. One day, at lunchtime, he sat near the fence where she was. The gardener had a banana that was overripe, and he brought it to give to the butterfly. So thoughtful. So as he sat eating his lunch, he just waited for the butterfly to join him, and she did.

"From that day on, they spent almost every day together. As the gardener would push the lawn mower, the butterfly would sit on his shoulder. He would hum and talk to the butterfly. One day, he was praying. The butterfly asked him what he was saying. He told her that he was praying for his family. The butterfly asked him, 'Just what do you mean by praying?'

"The gardener said, 'Come with me, I have something to show you.' She sat on his shoulder, and he walked to a little storage shed. He opened the door, and there was a beautiful cross on the wall. The butterfly asked, 'Why is that hanging on your wall?' He said, 'That, my sweet friend, is a cross. All though simple and stark, it holds very special meaning to Christians.' The butterfly looked sad, because she didn't understand what the gardener meant.

"The gardener picked up a book and said, 'This, my little friend, is my Bible. In this beautiful book are the answers to all your questions, from now until forever. It taught me how to live a faith-filled life. "The grass withers and the flowers fade, but the word of our God will stand forever," Isaiah 40:8.'

"'Can you show me and teach me?' asked the butterfly.

"'Yes, pleased and happy to,' he said. 'Let's start today, and together we will read this Bible from beginning to end, Mariposa.'

"'What does *Mariposa* mean?' she asked.

"'*Mariposa* means "butterfly" in Spanish. May I call you that?' the gardener asked.

"'Yes, please do.' She smiled back.

"'How do you say grandpa in Spanish?' she asked.

"'Abuelito, ab-ue-lito.' he said.

"'Can I call you Weto? It's easier for me to say.' she said.

"'Yes!' he implied with a smile. "'I would love that.'

"The gardener began, 'Genesis 1, The creation of the world. "In the beginning, God created the heavens and the earth. The earth was without form and void, and darkness was over the face of the deep. And the Spirit of God was hovering over the face of the waters."'

"So the gardener and the butterfly met every day for a year. They read chapter after chapter until they finished the entire Bible. Together they not only became very close friends but very knowledgeable about the blessed life our precious Lord had given them.

"To this day, that butterfly still reads her Bible and takes every available chance to share the gospel."

"That was a wonderful story, is it true?" asked the caterpillar.

"Oh yes, it is very true. And this is not the first time I've shared it." The butterfly smiled.

"I want to start right now, today. Where can I get a Bible? Will you show me, help me?" ranted the caterpillar.

"Yes, yes, yes, but slow down. I'm meeting with my friends, my four Prayer Pals, on Wednesday. Would you like to join us?" she asked.

"Oh *wow*, with your Prayer Pals! So they already know about the Bible?" he replied. "Are you sure they would want me there?"

"Yes!" And she reached out to touch him. He began to cry.

"If your God is anything like you, I already like him," answered the caterpillar.

"Okay, I'll let my friends know. We can all talk about John 3:16," she smiled.

"*What?* Did you say John?" he shrieked.

"Yes, is something wrong?" she asked.

"My name is John! Boy, I'm beginning to understand what you meant by blessings."

"Okay, John, we will meet you here at about ten on Wednesday morning.

CHAPTER 6

Returning Kindness

Early the next morning, John began his day by doing one of his favorite hobbies, woodworking. He gathered five small branches and looked around to find some long, sturdy grass. He had an idea about putting together five crosses for the Prayer Pals' visit.

He got everything all set up. He cut a short part off the top of the little branch and used it to lay over the longer piece, making a very small cross. Then he secured it with the grass. He polished each one and kept smiling the entire time he worked.

When the crosses were complete, he went for a walk just wondering what Wednesday was going to be like.

Mariposa flew to church, and there were her friends. They were sitting by the one window open on spring days. It was Carol's favorite place to sit. It was near the organ so we could sing or hum along to the hymns. But this morning, while waiting for the service to begin, Mariposa told the Prayer Pals about the great time spent with the caterpillar. They were so happy and really excited to meet and spend time with him on Wednesday.

"Oh, and ladies, I told him we would talk about John:3–16, and he was shocked because his name is John. What are the chances?" Mariposa said.

"Our sweet Lord never ceases to amaze," said Barb.

"What can we take him?" asked Miriam.

"I just finished a quilt he could lie on," said Carol.

"I can bake some apples to take," replied Susie.

"I am going to take a Bible to him," said Mariposa.

"I will take him a pillow," said Miriam.

"I could bring a jar of honey," replied Barb.

Just then, the church service began, so as the Prayer Pals listened, they were all smiling. And one of the hymns played was "Amazing Grace," a perfect song to hear that morning.

"Amazing grace, how sweet the sound that saved a wretch like me! I once was lost, but now I'm found; I once was blind, but now I see."

Chapter 7

Amazing Grace

John woke up early on Wednesday morning. He raked his area where he and the Prayer Pals were going meet. He was so excited to meet the butterfly friends and to start his walk with God. He pulled six nice-size leaves into a circle where they could sit comfortably and see one another's face easily. Then he carefully set a cross on five leaves. He placed a few pretty flowers in the middle. He stepped back to look, with a big smile on his face.

Just then, a frog jumps in between a tree and where John was standing.

"Good morning," said the frog. "I'm here to deliver a few thank-yous."

"Hi, my name is John. What's your name?" he asked.

"Frog."

"I know you are a frog, but what's your name?" John questioned.

"Yes, I am a frog, but the letters stand for Forever Rely On God, so that's what I was named." The frog smiled.

"Wow, that's great," remarked John.

"So I'm here to share a couple Bless-Yous," the frog began.

"A few days ago, I was just hopping around visiting friends when I came upon a bird friend. Her name is Colleen.

She told me the story about you helping her. She was so thankful. She wanted to tell you that she has been praying for you, but she didn't even know your name. Then yesterday, I saw a sweet lady friend, her name is Nancy. She told me that when she was taking her morning walk, she saw a dog tag in plain view.

She knew who it belonged to. She put it in an envelope and sent it to a wonderful lady named Kelly. It was the dog tag belonging to her all-time favorite dog, Georgia. Kelly, nicknamed the dog YaYa. She will be thrilled. 'I wish I knew who to thank for this show of kindness'.

"I heard from one of the Prayer Pals that they were coming to visit you this morning. I've heard some very nice stories about you lately. So I'm here to say hello, and I would enjoy getting to know you. My mom once said to me, 'Our Lord works in mysterious ways.' Boy, John, she was so right. It has been a blessing to meet you," the frog said.

They shook a couple of hands, and the frog hopped away.

It was just about time for the Prayer Pals to get together with him. John set out some water and just waited for his friend Mariposa and her friends to show up.

They all flew in together. Mariposa landed and next was Susie, who handed him some baked apples. Then Barb handed him a jar of honey.

"Oh my, this is so thoughtful. It is a gift having you visit and you bring gifts. Thank you all so very much," John said. "Please, find a comfy leaf to relax on."

Then Carol and Miriam stepped up and handed him a quilt and pillow. He began to cry. "I feel so undeserving of all of you coming to spend time with me, and also for the thoughtful gifts. How can I ever repay this?" he said.

Mariposa replied, "John, we have all been where you are. Nice kindnesses extended to us when we felt undeserving or others praying for us when we were too weak to speak. But when you become part of a family larger than you've ever known and share a Father who deeply loves us, it all begins to make precious sense. That's why we are all here today—to share that with you. Shall we all sit down?"

The Prayer Pals were just so moved by the beautiful crosses that John had made for them. Each one of them gave him a hug. Then Mariposa handed John a Bible. It had his name on the front. He hugged it and thanked them.

"John, each one of us highlighted some of our favorite verses and intitialed it," said the butterfly.

John said shyly, "Can I mark John 3:16, because I think I'm going to remember that one."

The Prayer Pals all laughed, and John joined in. The time went by so quickly—questions, answers, stories, old memories, new memories, it was just a wonderful day with friends. And as it says in the Bible, "Gracious words are like a honeycomb, sweetness to the soul and health to the body" (Proverbs 16:24).

As the day was coming to a close, Mariposa told John that he was welcome to join them every Wednesday and Sunday if he'd liked. She encouraged him to read his Bible and, if he had questions, to mark them in his book so they could all talk about it.

Then Mariposa said, "John, this is Barb, she brought the honey. She has blue wings. Then this is Carol, she brought the quilt. She has pink wings. And this is Miriam, she brought the pillow, and she has red wings. And this is Susie, she has orange wings, and she brought you the baked apples. John, do you have any more questions for today?"

He took a moment to look at each butterfly, then he said "Yes, thank you for introducing each butterfly, but you brought me my Bible, and I don't know your name."

"My name is Mariposa."

John looked surprised. "But the story about the lonely butterfly, that couldn't have been you?"

"Yes, John it was me. My first name is Barbara. Thanks to my wonderful Weto, my life was changed, and now I'm loved and never lonely. So I kept the name he called me. As Weto once said to me, 'You never have to be lonely, just talk to Jesus. I love you, but He loves you even more.' John, we want to thank you for the lovely crosses," said Mariposa.

"Oh, I want to thank you for crossing my path. And I understand you five being butterflies, but I truly believe that you five are betterflies because of your faith," John replied.

The six of them closed in prayer, giving all praise and glory to our precious Lord.

It's not the end. It's only the beginning!

31

ATA

Barbara Williamson writes with compassionate encouragement for children but in themes suitable for and enjoyed by all ages. In this, her sixth, book, she tells a story of the life-changing difference having a Bible and the knowledge of God in our lives makes. She shares a true story about the gardener, her Grandfather Weto, that made such a difference in her young life. She prays that all children hear a loving voice sharing God, prayer, and the Bible with them.

Barbara has an AA degree in sociology and experience in elementary school teaching. She is happily married to Sydney Williamson. She was blessed by a mom and grandpa with faith-filled hearts.

Visit her at www.talesofdeardreams.com.

ATB

This is a warm, inviting reflection of five Prayer Pals that never miss an opportunity to share their faith and prayers. Although each butterfly has her own story of how she came to know about God and the Bible, they now spend time together helping others. This is a view into just such a time shared with a lonely caterpillar.

Mariposa happens upon the caterpillar and befriends him. She shares with her Prayer Pals how lost he is and asks for their help to rescue him from his loneliness and introduce him to God and the Bible. They sweetly share a favorite Bible verse of their own. Together they make a plan to meet with the caterpillar and share their faith.

Mariposa candidly shares her personal story with the caterpillar. She was blessed by a caring, faith-filled heart, and so like all the Prayer Pals who have been blessed, it's now time for them to be a blessing to others.

Printed in the United States
by Baker & Taylor Publisher Services